leapfrog
Rhyme
Time

Felicity Floss: Tooth Fairy

by Maeve Friel

Illustrated by Sarah Horne

W
FRANKLIN WATTS
LONDON•SYDNEY

My name's Felicity Floss.
Hello!

I've been the tooth fairy
since ages ago.

My job is keeping
all of you happy,

while your smiles
are looking gappy.

But now I hear some
of you lisping:

"I've been wobbed!
My toof's gone missing!"

I must agree
it's not very funny,

10

to lose a tooth
and get no money.

11

But don't blame me, whatever you do!

I'm just as cross
as any of you!

So, last night, while you children slept,

I silently from my
toadstool crept ...

15

16

... to see for once
who was the thief,
stealing all your
pearly teeth.

17

I'd hardly left my fairy den to start my moonlit hunting, when ...

... down an alley
I heard a squeak

and saw a ratty
figure sneak ...

21

... nipping along on
tippy toes,
shiny white pearls
all over his clothes.

23

Shiny white pearls?
Could they be teeth?

24

"Oi! DJ Pearly! You're the milk teeth thief!"

"C...c...cool it, Fliss!"
the rat spat back.

"Gleaming like this is in my act!"

I whooshed my wand.
I said, "Take that!

To pay him back for
the teeth he took,
what did I do?
Well, just look!

Leapfrog has been specially designed to fit the requirements of the National Literacy Strategy. It offers real books for beginning readers by top authors and illustrators.

There are 43 Leapfrog stories to choose from:

The Bossy Cockerel
ISBN 0 7496 3828 1

Bill's Baggy Trousers
ISBN 0 7496 3829 X

Mr Spotty's Potty
ISBN 0 7496 3831 1

Little Joe's Big Race
ISBN 0 7496 3832 X

The Little Star
ISBN 0 7496 3833 8

The Cheeky Monkey
ISBN 0 7496 3830 3

Selfish Sophie
ISBN 0 7496 4385 4

Recycled!
ISBN 0 7496 4388 9

Felix on the Move
ISBN 0 7496 4387 0

Pippa and Poppa
ISBN 0 7496 4386 2

Jack's Party
ISBN 0 7496 4389 7

The Best Snowman
ISBN 0 7496 4390 0

Eight Enormous Elephants
ISBN 0 7496 4634 9

Mary and the Fairy
ISBN 0 7496 4633 0

The Crying Princess
ISBN 0 7496 4632 2

Jasper and Jess
ISBN 0 7496 4081 2

The Lazy Scarecrow
ISBN 0 7496 4082 0

The Naughty Puppy
ISBN 0 7496 4383 8

Freddie's Fears
ISBN 0 7496 4382 X

Cinderella
ISBN 0 7496 4228 9

The Three Little Pigs
ISBN 0 7496 4227 0

Jack and the Beanstalk
ISBN 0 7496 4229 7

The Three Billy Goats Gruff
ISBN 0 7496 4226 2

Goldilocks and the Three Bears
ISBN 0 7496 4225 4

Little Red Riding Hood
ISBN 0 7496 4224 6

Rapunzel
ISBN 0 7496 6159 3

Snow White
ISBN 0 7496 6161 5

The Emperor's New Clothes
ISBN 0 7496 6163 1

The Pied Piper of Hamelin
ISBN 0 7496 6164 X

Hansel and Gretel
ISBN 0 7496 6162 3

The Sleeping Beauty
ISBN 0 7496 6160 7

Rumpelstiltskin
ISBN 0 7496 6153 4*
ISBN 0 7496 6165 8

The Ugly Duckling
ISBN 0 7496 6154 2*
ISBN 0 7496 6166 6

Puss in Boots
ISBN 0 7496 6155 0*
ISBN 0 7496 6167 4

The Frog Prince
ISBN 0 7496 6156 9*
ISBN 0 7496 6168 2

The Princess and the Pea
ISBN 0 7496 6157 7*
ISBN 0 7496 6169 0

Dick Whittington
ISBN 0 7496 6158 5*
ISBN 0 7496 6170 4

Squeaky Clean
ISBN 0 7496 6588 2*
ISBN 0 7496 6805 9

Craig's Crocodile
ISBN 0 7496 6589 0*
ISBN 0 7496 6806 7

Felicity Floss: Tooth Fairy
ISBN 0 7496 6590 4*
ISBN 0 7496 6807 5

Captain Cool
ISBN 0 7496 6591 2*
ISBN 0 7496 6808 3

Monster Cake
ISBN 0 7496 6592 0*
ISBN 0 7496 6809 1

The Super Trolley Ride
ISBN 0 7496 6593 9*
ISBN 0 7496 6810 5

* hardback

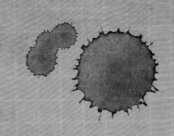
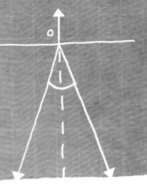

KT-447-435

This igloo book belongs to:

....

igloobooks

Published in 2019
by Igloo Books Ltd
Cottage Farm
Sywell
NN6 0BJ
www.igloobooks.com

Copyright © 2018 Igloo Books Ltd

All rights reserved. No part of this publication may be
reproduced or transmitted in any form or by any means,
electronic, or mechanical, including photocopying, recording,
or by any information storage and retrieval system,
without permission in writing from the publisher.

GUA006 0119
2 4 6 8 10 9 7 5 3
ISBN 978-1-78670-586-0

Written by Hannah Campling
Illustrated by Gareth Williams

Cover designed by Lee Italiano and Jason Shortland
Interiors designed by Jason Shortland
Edited by Caroline Richards

Printed and manufactured in China

WRITTEN BY
HANNAH CAMPLING

ILLUSTRATED BY
GARETH WILLIAMS

RACE TO THE MOON AND BACK

igloobooks

Next-door neighbours, Albert and Arthur, were as different as could be. Albert was neat, with a perfectly curled moustache and a spotless house.

ALBERT

Arthur was messy, with a bushy beard and a cluttered house full of cobwebs. They had just one thing in common. Albert and Arthur were both inventors.

One day, Albert heard a **CRASH** in next-door's garden. Looking up, he saw Arthur wobbling on a rickety ladder next to a strange machine. **"WHAT ON EARTH IS THAT?"** shouted Albert.

ARTHUR1

Albert **CRASHED** and **CLATTERED** as he scrambled to build his own spaceship. **"MINE'S ALMOST READY!"** shouted Arthur, cramming his ship with everything he might need.

Albert panicked and grabbed all of his best inventions. **"I'LL NEED MY SUPER-STICKY SPACE GLUE!"** Albert heard Arthur say. Albert laughed. **"YOUR GLUE IS RUBBISH. I'M PACKING MY MARVELLOUS MELTING MACHINE."**

MARVELLOUS
MELTING
MACHINE

At last, everything was ready.
The ground shook. The spaceships **ROARED**.

3... 2... 1...

... BLAST OFF!

With a **BLAST** of engines, Albert zoomed ahead... "NOT SO FAST!" yelled Arthur, as he pulled a **TURBO-BOOST** lever and sped into the lead.

Albert and Arthur raced neck-and-neck through the deep black sky and twinkling stars. They were so busy racing that they didn't see the Moon coming closer and closer, until...

THUD! CLATTER! SMASH!
The spaceships landed on the Moon.
The doors of both rockets **CLANGED**
open as Albert and Arthur tumbled out.

"I TOLD YOU MY SHIP WAS
THE BEST," said Albert.

A huge, green alien grabbed Arthur's spaceship. It sniffed it, then opened its mouth wide... and took a huge bite.

CRUNCH!

Albert's legs started to shake. Arthur wanted to run away. **"YUCK!"** spat the alien, and dropped the spaceship with a...

...THUD!

The alien snatched Albert's spaceship next,
and ate a mouthful of the roof.

"YUM, YUM!" it said, then it
slithered away and sat down to eat.

"OH, NO!" exclaimed Albert. "HOW ARE WE GOING TO GET HOME?"
"DON'T ASK ME," said Arthur. "THIS RACE WAS ALL YOUR IDEA."
"YOU STARTED IT!" argued Albert.

"IF YOU HADN'T BUILT THAT SILLY ROCKET, WE WOULDN'T BE IN THIS MESS."
Arthur was about to argue back, when a loud **SNORE** made them both jump.

The alien had finished eating and had fallen asleep. "WE HAVEN'T GOT TIME TO ARGUE," whispered Arthur. Albert nodded. "YOU'RE RIGHT," he said. "IF WE WORK TOGETHER, I'M SURE WE CAN MEND YOUR SPACESHIP AND GET HOME. I NEED MY MARVELLOUS MELTING MACHINE!"

The top of the spaceship had been broken into lots of pieces and the door had been torn away. So, Albert used his Marvellous Melting Machine and Arthur found his Super-Sticky Space Glue.

They used the space glue to mend the door and fitted it to the gap with a **CLANG!**

Next, Albert and Arthur **HAMMERED** the pieces of the spaceship back together, like a giant jigsaw puzzle.

Suddenly, a loud **GROWL** shook the ground. They looked at the alien. It yawned. One eye flickered open. **"QUICK!"** yelled Albert. The alien was wide awake and wiggling closer and closer.

Albert and Arthur scrambled into the spaceship
and pulled the door shut with a **CLANG.**

They quickly pressed the big red button and **... BLAST OFF!**

As they watched the alien disappear into the distance, Arthur said, **"RIGHT, LET'S GO HOME."** Albert looked out into space.

"WHY DON'T WE EXPLORE ANOTHER PLANET INSTEAD?" he said.

Arthur grinned. "YES, LET'S GO ON ANOTHER ADVENTURE!"

He pulled the turbo lever and they **ZOOMED** towards the stars.

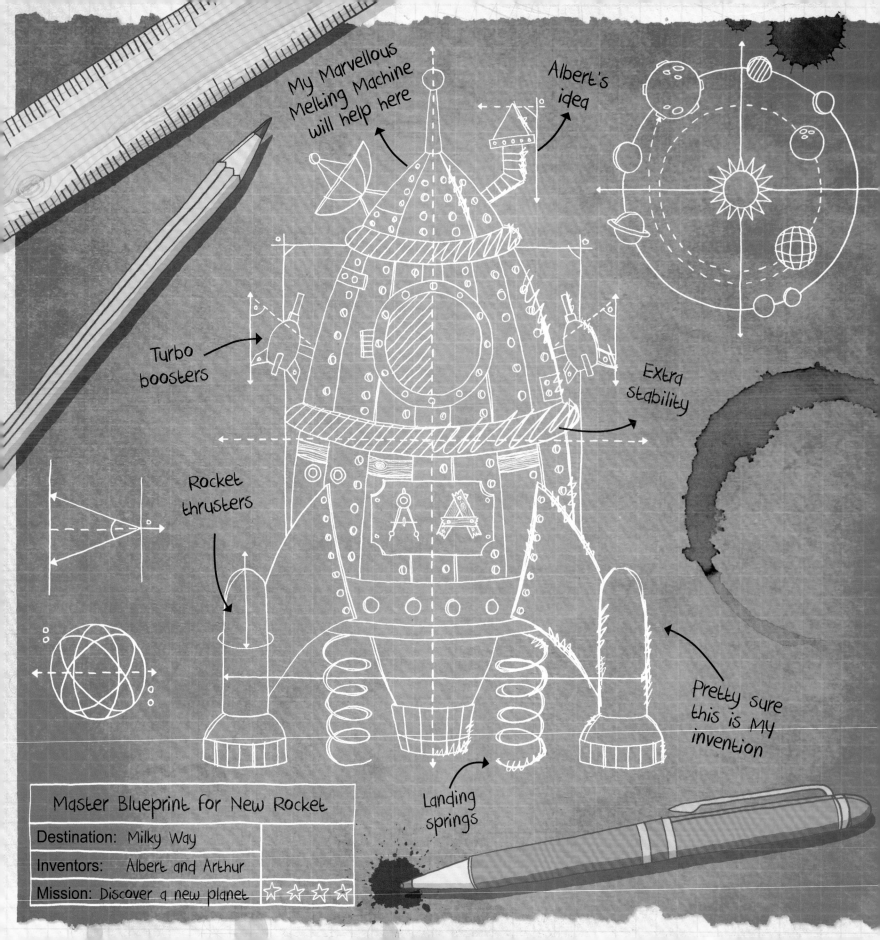